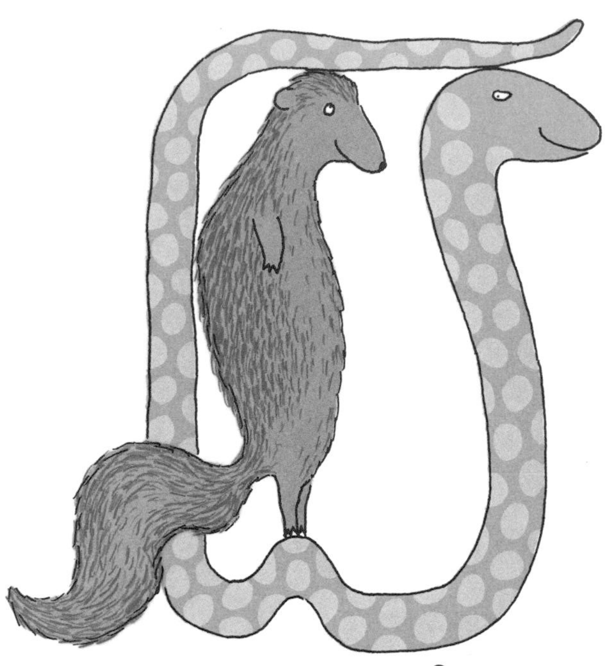

Marie Louise & Christophe

by Natalie Savage Carlson

pictures by Jose Aruego & Ariane Dewey

CHARLES SCRIBNER'S SONS, NEW YORK

1 3 5 7 9 11 13 15 17 19 RD/C 20 18 16 14 12 10 8 6 4 2
Printed in the United States of America
Library of Congress Catalog Card Number 73-19365
ISBN 0-684-13736-4

For my first great-grandchild,
Cristina Marie Williamson

Marie Louise was a little brown mongoose. She looked something like a squirrel but more like a mink. She lived with her mama in a thatched hut in a field of sugarcane.
Her best friend was a little spotted green snake named Christophe. She played with him almost every day. But sometimes he played tricks on her.

One day Christophe said, “Let us play hide-and-seek in the sugarcane forest. I’ll cover my eyes and you hide.”

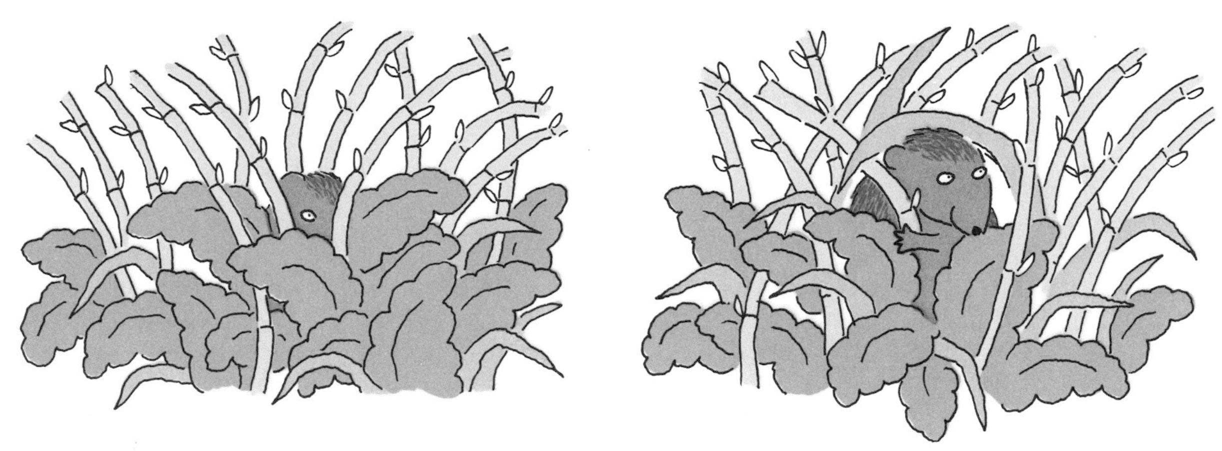

Marie Louise hid herself behind a clump of cane stalks. She waited and waited.

“What a good hiding place I’ve found,” she told herself. She waited some more.

“Perhaps I have found too good a hiding place,” she told herself. “Christophe can’t find me.”

She went back to find Christophe, but he had gone home.
"I couldn't find you," he told her later.

"I don't think you even looked for me,"
said Marie Louise. "It's just one of your tricks."

Next day Christophe said, “I am long and thin like a rope. I will make a swing for you.”

He hooked his head and tail over a low branch.

Marie Louise sat in the swing he made. She began pumping up.

She went higher and higher.

Suddenly Christophe let go with his tail.

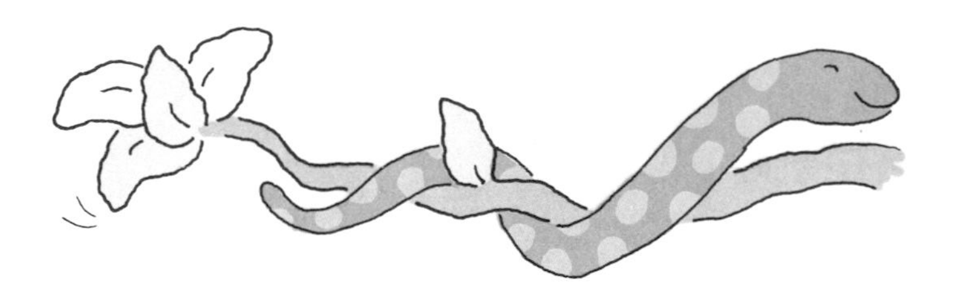

Marie Louise fell on the ground.
"Oh, Oh!" said Christophe. "My tail must have slipped."

"I think you did it on purpose,"
said Marie Louise. "It was one of your tricks."

Next day Marie Louise's mama said to her, "I am going to bake a cake. Go to the mill and fetch me a sack of sticky brown sugar. But be careful the Man doesn't see you take it."

At a fork in the path, Marie Louise met Christophe. "Where are you going?" he asked.

"To the mill to get a sack of sticky brown sugar for my mama," said Marie Louise.

"I will go with you," said Christophe. " I will watch out for the Man so you will be safe."
They went up the path to the mill together.

Christophe watched out for the Man while Marie Louise filled her sack with sugar.

She took a lick from it, then offered him a lick.
It tasted like flowers smell.

As they started back, Christophe said,
"You walk ahead. I'll come behind so I can see
that the Man isn't following us."
Marie Louise went ahead with the sack of sugar
balanced on her head.

After awhile she sat down to rest in the shade of the sugarcane. Christophe sat down beside the sack. He nibbled a hole in it when Marie Louise wasn't looking.

"I'm rested now," said Marie Louise. "Let's be on our way." As she walked along, the sticky brown sugar slowly spilled onto the path. Christophe licked it up as he followed.

Marie Louise soon noticed that the sack on her head was very light. She took it down. It was empty. She saw the hole that Christophe had nibbled.

She was very angry. "You aren't my friend anymore," she said. "You are my enemy."

Christophe stuck out his forked tongue at her. "Then you are my enemy," he said. "Someday we shall have the big fight and I will beat you!"

Marie Louise raised all her hair on end so she would look bigger. "Someday we shall have the big fight," she said, "but *I* will beat *you!*"

Marie Louise's mama was angry because she didn't bring the sugar home. She raised all her own hair on end.

"You will have to go back to the mill tomorrow for the sticky brown sugar," she said. "I will wait to bake the cake."

Next day Marie Louise went up the path through
the sugarcane. She met Christophe at the fork.

"You can't come with me," she told him. "You are my enemy."

Christophe stuck out his forked tongue at her.

“I’m not afraid of you,” Christophe said. “If it wasn’t for that pretty tail, you would only be a rat.”

Marie Louise raised every hair on end.
“I’m not afraid of you,” she said. “If it wasn’t for that pretty skin, you would only be a worm.”

Christophe said, "Someday we shall have the big fight and I will beat *you!* I am very fierce. This morning I beat up a fighting cock."

Marie Louise said, "Someday we shall have the big fight and I will beat *you!* I am very fierce, too. This morning I beat up a snake twice as big as you."

Marie Louise went on up the path through the sugarcane to the mill.
When the Man wasn't looking, she filled another sack
with sticky brown sugar.

On the way back, she stopped three times to take a lick
of the sugar that tasted like flowers smell.

But Marie Louise didn't go straight home.
She climbed up a steep hill to the Witch Toad's house under a big black rock.
The ugly Witch Toad was at home. "What do you want, my pretty mongoose maid?" he asked. "I make good luck charms and bad luck charms. Sometimes I make charms that have no luck."

Marie Louise said, "I have a bad enemy who wants to fight me. I need a charm to protect me from him."

"I have just the right charm," said the Witch Toad, "but what will you pay me?"

"This sticky brown sugar with only one lick missing," said Marie Louise.

The Witch Toad snatched the sack from her.
He looked inside.
"You are not telling me the truth," he scolded. "There are three licks missing. But I will give you the charm anyway."

He ducked under the big rock for a few seconds.
When he appeared again, he handed her the charm.
Marie Louise looked at it doubtfully.
"It is only a blackbird's feather," she said.

"But it is full of magic," said the Witch Toad.

"Only a short while ago I sold such a charm to a
little green snake. He has a bad enemy, too."
So Marie Louise was satisfied.
She hurried down the steep hill for home.

She met Christophe again at the fork in the path.
She quickly hid her charm. He quickly hid his.
Marie Louise said, "I'm not afraid of you.
When we have the big fight, I am sure to win."

Christophe said, "And I'm not afraid of you because I know for sure that I will win the big fight."

Marie Louise's mama was angry when she found that the sticky brown sugar had been traded for a charm. The charm did not protect Marie Louise from her mama's spanking.
Her mama said, "Tomorrow you must go back to the mill for another sack of sticky brown sugar. And mind you bring it home this time."

So next day Marie Louise started out for the mill once more. She held tightly to her charm. She hid it when she met Christophe at the fork.

"Have you seen the pretty playhouse
the Man has made for you?" said Christophe.

"What pretty playhouse?" asked Marie Louise. "My mama
didn't say anything about it."

"It is a pretty playhouse woven of grasses,"
said Christophe. "I'll show it to you."

He led her through the stalks of sugarcane to a pretty little
woven hut. Marie Louise was delighted.
"It is the prettiest playhouse I've ever seen," she said.

“The door is open.” Christophe pointed. “Go inside.
It’s even prettier there.”
Marie Louise went through the doorway.

Click! The door closed. She was caught inside!

“Aha!” cried Christophe. “It isn’t a playhouse at all.
It’s a trap the Man set for you.”

He said no more because suddenly a big basket fell over him.

He was caught in a trap, too!

The Man came that evening. He slipped a cover
on the basket. He carried it and the woven hut
to his village near the sugar mill.

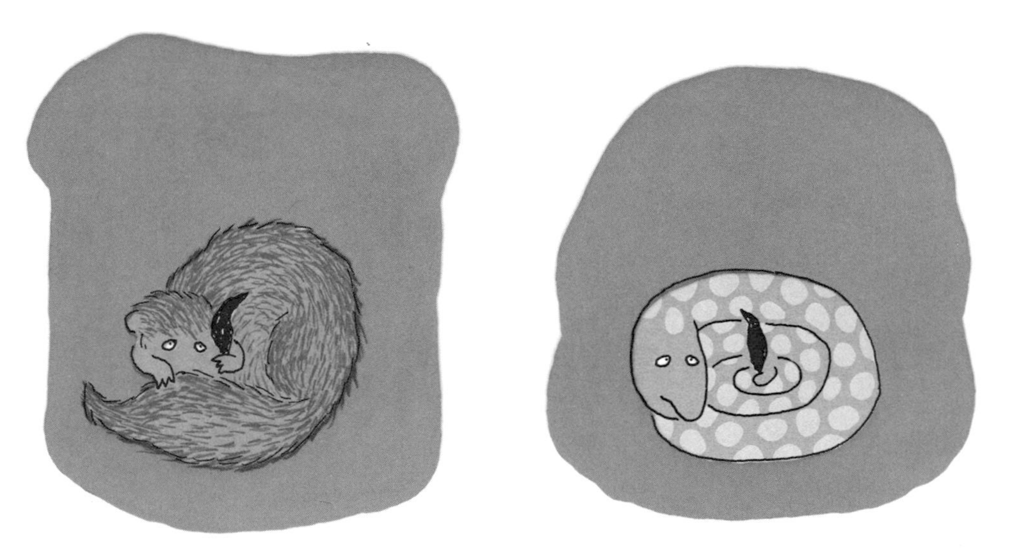

Marie Louise was frightened. She clutched her charm
tightly, but it didn't to anything to free her. She didn't
know what had happened to Christophe. She thought he had
run home after playing his biggest trick on her.
Christophe was frightened, too. He curled himself
around his charm, but it didn't do anything to free him.

Next day the Man put Marie Louise in a big screened cage.
There was a crowd of men squatting around the cage.
"And now, gentlemen," the Man cried, "you will see a fierce fight between a mongoose and a snake."
He opened the door of the cage and who should slide in but Christophe!
"That is only a little snake," grumbled one of the men.
"And the mongoose is little, too," cried another.
"But they are deadly enemies," the Man shouted. "They will now fight to the death!"

Marie Louise began to shiver and shake.
"I don't want to fight you," she told Christophe.

Christophe began to shiver and shake.
"And I don't want to fight you," he said. "I only said
I would beat you in the big fight so you would be afraid of me."

"I only said I would beat you
so you would be afraid of *me*," said Marie Louise.

"I didn't really beat up a fighting cock," said Christophe.

"And I didn't really beat up a snake twice as big as you,"
said Marie Louise.

"I only led you into the trap so you would never be able to fight me," said Christophe. "But now the Man says we must have the big fight."

"We don't have to do what the Man says," said Marie Louise. "Let's not fight the big fight."

"The Man is really our enemy," said Christophe. "Let's be friends again."

So Marie Louise sat down on the floor of the cage.
Christophe gently coiled around her .
They stared at the men squatting around the cage.

The men were angry.
"They're not going to fight," cried one.
"They act more like friends," cried another.
The men shook their fists at the Man.
"Give us our money back," they cried.
The Man was angry, too. He gave the cage a great kick.

It went rolling over and over. Marie Louise and
Christophe went rolling over and over with it.
The cage struck the trunk of a palm tree.
The door flew open.
Marie Louise and Christophe crawled out.

They raced away from the village as fast
as they could. They didn't stop until they
were back in the field of sugarcane.

"I'm sorry I played tricks on you,"
said Christophe. "I'll never make you fall from my swing again."

"It really didn't hurt me," said Marie Louise.

"And I'll never play hide-and-seek again the way I did,"
said Christophe.

"It didn't matter," said Marie Louise. "It was cool
and pleasant hiding in the sugarcane."

"And I'll never eat your sugar again," said Christophe.

"I don't blame you," said Marie Louise. "I like to lick
the sticky brown sugar, too. It tastes like flowers smell."

So they threw their charms away and went home together.